Billy
Rubbish

Also by Alexander McCall Smith

Akimbo and the Crocodile Man
Akimbo and the Elephants
Akimbo and the Lions
Spaghetti Tangle
Who Invented Peanut Butter?

First published in Great Britain 1995
by Methuen Children's Books Ltd
Published 1996 by Mammoth
an imprint of Reed International Books Ltd
Michelin House, 81 Fulham Road, London SW3 6RB
and Auckland, Melbourne, Singapore and Toronto

Reprinted 1997

ISBN 0 7497 2596 6

A CIP catalogue record for this title
is available from the British Library

Printed and bound in Great Britain
by Cox & Wyman Ltd, Reading, Berkshire

Alexander McCall Smith
Billy Rubbish

illustrated by
Martin Chatterton

For Stephen Davidson

CONTENTS

1. The Messiest Town of All

Unlike most of the people who lived in his town, Billy was not a messy person. In fact, Billy was quite neat, and he never threw litter down on the street or dumped things when he had finished with them. But even so, he had been so used to living there that he hardly noticed the mess. He did not really see the fields full of abandoned cars, or the old refrigerators lying half in, half out of the stream. Nor did he see the rusty old bed, which somebody had thrown away, and sometimes had a pig lying on it in sunny weather. And of course, he hardly even minded the lumps of chewing gum which would stick to your shoes as you walked along.

Then, one day Billy got a real shock. There, in the middle of the front page of the newspaper, was a photograph of his town! At first, Billy was rather proud to see it, but as he read what was written below, the smile faded from his face.

'This is a picture of the messiest town in the country. It has been awarded the prize in our annual competition to find the messiest town of all. It won over five hundred votes from people who had been there. So, well done, or rather, badly done!'

Billy's jaw dropped. How terrible! What a dreadful, embarrassing thing this was for the town! And it got worse as the report continued.

'Don't visit this town in your best clothes. You get messy just by walking along the street. And whatever you do, don't sit on any of the town benches, if you can find any of them under the mess! They haven't been cleaned for years so your clothes will get covered with grime. And here's another piece of advice if you're unfortunate enough to have to go there: take a clothes peg to put on your nose. Yes! The town smells!'

Billy could hardly believe what he read. Was it his own town that they were talking about, or was it some other place in some other far off country? He checked the picture. No, it was definitely his town which had been chosen for this dreadful prize. The thought horrified him. He had always been proud of his town and thought it was a good place to live, but now he felt nothing but shame.

He cut out the picture and the report, tucked it in his pocket, and left the house. He went straight down to the town hall and asked to see the mayor.

'Look at this,' said Billy, handing the mayor the report. 'Have you seen what's in the newspaper today?'

The mayor took the piece of paper from Billy and read it silently. Then he looked up – and shrugged his shoulders.

'Ted should be ashamed of himself,' he said. 'In fact, I'm going to dismiss

him. It's no good having somebody who doesn't do his job properly. It would be cheaper to have nobody at all!'

Ted was the local street sweeper. He had a shabby blue uniform and a cap which had lost its badge. It was his job to keep the town tidy but, however hard he worked, he couldn't even begin to clean up all the mess. It would take fifty, no, perhaps one hundred and fifty, street sweepers to clean up everything. And they would all have to work non-stop all week.

Billy could hardly believe what he was hearing. Here was the mayor blaming Ted – just as everybody always did – and now poor Ted was going to lose his job!

And there was another surprise in store. When the mayor had read the report, he crumpled it up into a ball and threw it down on the ground – just like that! Billy stood quite still in his astonishment. Then, very slowly, he reached forward and picked up the piece of paper. But the mayor, I'm afraid to say, didn't even notice.

Billy walked home silently. It seemed as if nobody else cared very much, but he certainly did. And sometimes, when nobody else seems to care, it takes just one person to do something. Just one person.

2. Billy and the Waste Paper

Over the next few days, Billy spent a lot of time thinking. He realised that it was no good trying to tell people to make less mess, because they didn't seem to pay much attention. And if they did listen, then they just blamed Ted. Now that Ted had lost his job they might find that difficult, but they would be sure to come up with some other excuse.

'If we still had Ted,' they would say. 'Things wouldn't be so bad. It's the mayor's fault, you see. He shouldn't have dismissed him.'

Then they would shrug their shoulders and start to talk about something else.

Billy went to see Ted, and told him

how sorry he was that he had lost his job.

'Thank you,' said Ted, touched by Billy's concern. 'I'm quite pleased about it actually. I was about to give it up anyway. I've bought myself some pigs and I'm looking after them. It's much easier, actually. They're not so messy.'

'But surely we can do something,' said Billy. 'Surely we could make people change.'

Ted laughed. 'Change? That lot? There's no chance of that, I'm afraid. They're just messy and wasteful by nature!'

Billy was silent for a moment. 'Wasteful?' he asked.

'Yes,' said Ted. 'Look at all the stuff they throw away. If only they realised how much money they could save. That would give them something to think about!'

Ted paused. He could see that Billy was smiling, as if he had just had a good idea.

'I think I've thought of something,' said Billy slowly. 'Ted, what do you think is the biggest rubbish problem we have in this town?'

Ted looked thoughtful. 'Well, I've always hated those old cars and the dumped refrigerators, but I suppose it's paper. Yes, it must be paper. Old newspapers. They're the worst. They blow all over the place, even if you put them in the rubbish dump.'

'I see,' said Billy. 'And if we somehow managed to get people to do something with them, then would that make a difference?'

'It certainly would,' said Ted. 'It would make all the difference in the world. But I'm going to have to go now, Billy. I've got my pigs to feed.'

Billy said goodbye to Ted and then went home, thinking hard all the way. His idea was shaping up rather well, he felt. Now all that he had to do was to put it into operation. That, he knew, would be the hardest part.

Yet it did not take as long as he thought it would. The next morning, a Saturday, Billy went off to the library and found the directory he was looking for. It was a thick yellow book, with page after page of information about all the businesses in the area and what they did. Billy wanted a waste paper dealer. Of course there was nobody who did that in his messy town, but he soon found that there were four or five

dealers in nearby towns. It was not difficult to choose: Button and Brace, Waste Paper Dealers were the obvious people. They proclaimed in their advertisement: *Distance no object! You collect the paper; we collect from you; we recycle; you collect from us*!

Billy was interested. The first part was clear enough, but what did they mean when they said *'you collect from us'*? Surely you didn't get the paper back – there would be no point in that?

Billy jotted down their address on a piece of paper and went home. His younger sister, Nicola, always had a supply of writing paper, and she agreed to give him a piece.

'Who are you writing to?' she asked. 'You never write letters.'

'It's a business letter,' said Billy.

And with that he retired to his room, closed the door, and sat down at his desk.

Dear Mr Button and Mr Brace,

I hope that I shall shortly have a large number of old newspapers to be collected for recycling. Could you please come and collect them? And by the way, what do you mean when you say that we collect from you? What do we collect from you? Could you please explain.

He signed his name neatly, addressed the envelope, and went off to the post office to post his letter.

Over the next few days, Billy waited anxiously for his reply, and at last it came. It was in an envelope which had printed on it:

RECYCLED STATIONERY: NO TREES DIED!
BUTTON AND BRACE — WASTE PAPER DEALERS.

Billy opened the envelope carefully — he could use it again — and read the letter inside.

Dear Billy,

Thank you for writing to us. You have made a good choice. We're certainly the best people in the waste paper business around these parts. It's funny, though, that you're the first person to get in touch with us from your town. What's going on there? Have you not got the recycling bug yet?

Yes, we'll take your paper from you, and we'll turn it back into paper again! And in return, we'll give you supplies of recycled stationery, with your name and address printed at the top of each piece of paper. We find that people like that.

Let us know when the paper's ready and we'll be there!
Yours truly,
Button and Brace.

And underneath it said, in large red letters:
REMEMBER — DON'T THROW THIS LETTER AWAY! EVERY LITTLE COUNTS!

Billy smiled as he read the letter. It was exactly right for what he wanted to do, and now he could begin. It was the beginning of the end for the litter louts in the town (which was just about everybody). They didn't know it yet, but things were about to change!

3. Start Collecting!

The first thing that Billy had to do was to make the posters. He decided that Nicola might like to help him with this, and so he told her all about his plan.

'We have to collect lots and lots of old newspapers,' he said to his sister. 'We couldn't possibly collect all of these ourselves. We need to get other people to do it as well. And other people, as you know, often won't do things unless you give them a reason.'

Nicola nodded. 'I know,' she said. 'But how could we get people to collect papers. We can't afford to pay them.'

'We offer a prize,' said Billy. 'We offer a big prize.'

Nicola looked doubtful, but as Billy

explained to her what he had in mind, she became quite excited.

'That's a wonderful idea,' she said. 'Of course it'll work, Billy!'

So together the two of them sat down at the kitchen table and started to write out the posters which they would put up in school.

'Collect old newspapers and win – a mystery prize!' they wrote in large letters. 'Bring your newspapers to us and we'll weigh them. Then, after a week, the person who's brought the most will get a mystery prize that will be really worth having! So don't delay – start collecting!'

They made five of these posters. Next day Billy went to see one of the teachers and explained the scheme, and was quickly given permission to put up the posters.

'What a good idea,' said the teacher. 'In fact, it's about time that somebody started to do something about the mess in his town. Well done!'

The teacher thought for a moment. 'Where are you going to put all these papers before they come to collect them?' she asked. 'Have you got room at home?'

Billy said that he thought that he would put them in the garage at home, but the teacher suggested that it would be better to store them at the school.

'You can use one of the empty classrooms,' she said. 'There'll be much more room there.'

The posters went up that morning and after school, Billy saw an excited bunch

of people clustered around one of them.

'I'm going to win,' he heard one boy say to the others. 'My dad is really messy. We've got tons of old papers hanging about the house.'

'My mum's even messier,' said another. 'We've got old newspapers piled up under the kitchen table. You can't even get your feet under it. You won't win, I will.'

Billy slipped away, pleased that the competition had aroused such interest. Now all that he had to do was to wait for the following morning.

It started well. The next morning, Billy and Nicola were at the school gates with the bathroom scales which they had borrowed from their mother. They did not have long to wait, as they had barely arrived before they saw the first person come with a large pile of papers under his arm.

'Weigh these,' said the boy. 'And I've got bags more at home. I'll bring them

in tomorrow and the day after.'

As each pile of newspapers arrived,
Billy and Nicola put them on the scales
and noted down the weight in a little
book. It was hard work, and it was even
harder work taking all the papers up to
the empty classroom, but by the time
the school bell went for the beginning of
classes they had neatly stacked the

papers in the classroom and had tidied everything up.

The following day, the same thing happened, though this time word had really got around, and there were more and more people bringing in more and more papers. In the classroom, the pile of papers grew higher and higher.

'By the end of the week the classroom will be full,' said Nicola. 'What will we do then?'

Billy asked the teacher, who thought for a moment before she replied.

'There's another spare classroom,' she said. 'And there's also the gym. Perhaps we could get permission to start filling the gym. After all, this is a great service that you're doing the town.'

Over the next few days, the pile of newspapers grew and grew. They had been told that they were allowed to start putting them in the other classroom, and soon this, too, was almost full. Then they went on to the gym, and soon there was a mountain of newspapers there too.

'This is amazing,' said the school principal when she saw what was happening. 'To think that all these old papers were just sitting about in people's homes or in the streets! Why on earth did nobody think of collecting them before?'

Gradually, though, the supply of newspapers began to dwindle. Now was the time to get in touch with Button and Brace to tell them to come and collect the waste paper, but before he wrote to them, he and Nicola added up the totals to see who had collected the most.

There were three people who came very close to one another, but the person who had brought in just a little bit more than anybody else was Lucy, a girl in Nicola's class. Somehow Lucy had managed to bring in almost five hundred kilos of newspapers, which she had gathered from all her neighbours and all her neighbours' friends.

Billy wrote out her name and address on the bottom of his letter to Button and

Brace, and then slipped it into the recycled envelope in which their letter to him had arrived.

'Now we just have to wait,' he said to Nicola. 'With any luck we shall be able to announce the winner next week.'

Button and Brace wrote back a few days later, telling Billy when they would arrive at the school to collect the paper. Their letter came in the same envelope as before, which Billy had sent back to them, now stuck up with tape.

Billy showed the letter to the principal, who agreed that there could be an official prize giving when Button and Brace arrived. Everybody at the school would be there to watch both the prize giving and the carting away of the newspaper mountain.

And it was a grand occasion. Button and Brace came in a large van – made entirely out of recycled metal, of course – and shook Billy by the hand. Billy smiled as he looked at the two waste paper dealers, who were dressed in well-patched old clothes.

'Yes,' said Mr Button, noticing Billy's gaze, 'my shirts are entirely made of recycled old sheets. And my jacket used to be a bedspread.'

'Very good,' said the principal. 'I've got an old bedspread at home. You've given me an idea.'

Everybody in the school made a human chain to get the wastepaper into Button and Brace's old van. Newspapers were passed from hand to hand until every last scrap of paper was loaded. Then the principal addressed the school.

'Well done, everybody,' she said. 'This has been a splendid effort. But you'll all be waiting for the name of the winner of this competition, and Billy has given that to me on this scrap of recycled paper.'

She reached into her pocket and took out the winner's name. There was a great cheer as Lucy stood up.

'Well, Mr Button,' said the principal.

'Billy tells me that you've brought the prize with you.'

Mr Button nodded, and opened the cab of his van to extract a large box.

'Here it is,' he said. 'A year's supply of recycled stationery, printed with the winner's name and address. Congratulations!'

Everybody cheered again as Lucy received her prize. Then the principal signalled for everybody to be quiet and made an announcement.

'Now, listen to this,' she said. 'Just because we've collected all the old paper lying around doesn't mean that there won't be any more waste paper in the future. This competition is going to be an annual one. Mr Button will come here every month and collect any old newspapers you bring in, and at the end of the year he will give a box of recycled stationery to every member of the school. So three cheers for Mr Button!'

Billy was extremely pleased. The town looked much neater now, yet there was still a lot of unsightly metal lying around. That night, as he lay in bed thinking of the waste paper triumph, he realised that there was more work to be done. But exactly how it could be done was still puzzling.

4. The Rubbish Bin Competition

It was Nicola who solved the problem. She explained her idea to Billy the very next day over breakfast.

'We may have cleared up all the old newspapers,' she said. 'But what about all the old tins you see lying around? They're even more messy.'

Billy thought of all the old tins that you could find at the bottom of everybody's garden and the town dump, where people were meant to throw their rubbish. That was always piled high with tin cans.

'How can we get people to hand in their tins?' he asked. 'Newspapers are easy. Tins are dirty.'

Nicola smiled. 'I've had an idea. We

can telephone Mr Button . . .'

'He only collects newspapers,' broke in Billy. 'He won't want old tins.'

'But he's bound to have a friend who will want them,' retorted Nicola. 'You saw how keen he was on recycling. I bet he doesn't throw his old tins away.'

Billy thought for a moment. His sister was right – Mr Button would certainly help them if he could. But there was still the problem of how to get people to collect tins.

It was as if Nicola had guessed what

her brother was thinking.

'And it won't be hard to get people to collect them,' she said defiantly. 'Not if we have another competition.'

'But what can people get from old tins?' Billy asked. 'You can't make stationery out of them.'

'Rubbish bins,' said Nicola firmly. 'We'll have a rubbish bin competition.'

Billy listened intently as his sister explained her idea.

'We'll have a competition,' she said. 'Everybody who has collected at least one hundred tins will be able to enter. They'll be asked to design a rubbish bin!'

'And then?' asked Billy.

'Mr Button's friend will melt down some of the tins to make new rubbish bins for the town,' she said. 'And once the new bins are set up, I'm sure people will be a little bit tidier.'

'Who will be the judge?' he asked.

Nicola thought for a moment. 'Mr Button's friend?' she said. 'A rubbish man should know all about rubbish bins.'

Billy thought the whole thing a very good idea. 'And it will also mean that we'll have to use up less of the tin that's left in the world,' he said.

'Exactly,' said his sister.

Later that day, Billy phoned Mr Button. It was just as they had expected. Mr Button did have a friend who melted down old metal and used it again.

'Freddy Silver's your man!' said Mr Button, enthusiastically. 'Old Freddy will make anything out of old metal – anything!'

'Even from old tins?' asked Billy.

'Smelly old tins that may still have a few baked beans left in them?'

'No problem!' said Mr Button. 'You go ahead and collect them, and I'll bring old Freddy down to pick them up in his truck when you're ready.'

Billy and Nicola immediately sat down to make the posters announcing the competition. Then they went down to the town hall and pinned them up on a notice board, in a prominent place. Of course, word got round quickly. Everybody had enjoyed the paper collecting competition, and they were thrilled that here was another challenge.

People were told to be very careful in collecting tins. Very old tins, with sharp edges, were to be left where they were – they would rust away eventually. But all tins from the kitchen were to be saved – even if they still had some baked beans in them – and put into sacks.

'We've got at least fifty tins,' said one of Billy's friends. 'Our cat's greedy, you see. It eats tins and tins of cat food every day.'

'And I've got two hundred!' said another. 'My grandmother eats tinned asparagus all day – that's all she ever eats. You should see the pile of tins!'

Everybody was also very excited at the thought of designing rubbish bins. All over town, people got out paper and pencil and began to sketch out how they thought the bins should look. And while they were doing this, they made sure that every tin in the kitchen was neatly put into a sack, ready for collection.

By the next week, there was not a tin to

be seen lying around anywhere. People were beginning to pester Billy to collect their sacks. Billy telephoned Mr Button, who said that he and Freddy Silver would come the next morning.

Mr Button and Freddy Silver arrived early. Billy looked out of the kitchen window and saw a most peculiar truck draw up in front of their house. It looked as if it was made from lots of different sorts of metals, and it was all sorts of different colours. When he looked at it more closely he saw, to his astonishment, that it was made entirely out of tin cans, all welded together.

And as for Freddy Silver, he was a most impressive recycling person! He wore a wonderful belt, with a recycled door knob serving as the buckle. His cuff links were made out of old brass buttons, and attached to his ears were two shining curtain rings. And as for his tie-pin, that was nothing more than an old spoon, neatly twisted round, polished, and doing the job very well indeed!

Freddy smiled at Billy, showing some wonderful gold teeth.

'You and your sister can come round with us, if you like,' he said. 'You could help with all the sacks.'

The four of them set off in the peculiar truck. While Billy helped carry the sacks from the houses, Nicola collected people's drawings – once they were satisfied that they had collected at least one hundred tins from each house. It was hard work, and it took almost all day, but at the end of it Freddy's truck was almost completely full.

'There must have been a lot of old tins lying around,' said Freddy, wiping his face with his handkerchief. 'We've got tons of metal in the back there.'

They drove home, where Billy's mother had baked a large cake for them. While Mr Button and Freddy chatted in the kitchen, Nicola laid out all the drawings on the floor of the sitting room. Then she invited Freddy to be the judge.

'You choose,' she said, 'because you'll be making the bins.'

Freddy wiped his face again, and smiled his flashing gold smile. Then he wandered around the drawings, peering at each one closely, smiling over some and shaking his head over others. Then he stopped.

'Yes,' he muttered under his breath. Then, more loudly: 'Yes! Yes! This is the one!'

They all rushed over to look at the drawing, which Freddy had picked up

and was waving in the air. It was a very peculiar design indeed, but they all knew that Freddy had chosen just the right one.

'Are you sure you could make those?' asked Billy doubtfully.

'Of course I can,' retorted Freddy. 'And you'll have twenty of them delivered to the town hall next Saturday morning at ten o'clock. On the dot!'

Freddy was as good as his word. At precisely ten o'clock the following

Saturday, the peculiar old truck rolled into town and stopped in front of the town hall. Billy had told the mayor that the town would be receiving a present then and he had been thrilled.

'I love an occasion,' the mayor had said. 'I shall wear my chain of office and my new hat. And I shall make a speech. I'm rather good at that, you know.'

The mayor was also as good as his word. As the truck drew to a halt outside the town hall, he came out of the front door wearing his chain and his hat. And he had even cleaned the chain, which sparkled in the morning sun.

A large crowd of people was waiting anxiously. Everybody who had entered the competition was there, all sure that their design would be the winner.

Freddy opened the back door of his truck and everybody was silent.

'Ladies and Gentlemen,' said the mayor, who had become quite keen on recycling when he saw that everybody was doing it. 'This . . . er . . . this . . . this

gentleman here ... Mr Fred ... er ...
Freddy ... er ... Freddy Tin ... I mean
Freddy Silver has kindly made us new
rubbish bins for the town, and I ...
er ... being the sort of mayor who
believes in a clean town, thought that it
would be a great honour – no, I mean a
very ... er ... great honour to
announce ...'

'Come on!' muttered somebody. 'We
can't wait much longer.'

But at that moment, Freddy had
produced the first rubbish bin from the
back and there came a cry from the
crowd.

'It's mine!' shouted a girl called Holly,
who had been standing at the back. 'I
designed that!'

It was a wonderful bin. It was made in
the shape of an elephant's head, and
when you lifted the trunk, the top
opened, to allow the rubbish to be put
in. And the next one which Freddy took
out, also from the same design, was in

the shape of a pelican. With this one, you lifted the beak and popped in the rubbish. All the others, were each in the shape of animals' heads.

Everybody was thrilled, and cheered Holly for her clever design. They also cheered Freddy, for making the bins out of old tins. And they cheered Nicola, whose idea it had all been, and Billy, who had organised the competition. Then, when all the cheering was over, the mayor showed people exactly where the bins should be put, and he ceremoniously put in the first piece of rubbish.

'With bins like this,' he said. 'Everybody will be wanting to put their rubbish away.' And with that, he bent down, picked up a piece of paper from the ground, and popped it into the bin.

'I shall be doing a lot of that in the future,' said the mayor. 'And I hope everybody else picks up rubbish too! This town, I'm telling you, is going to change!'

One person in the crowd was particularly happy. It was Ted, the street sweeper turned pig keeper.

'I can hardly believe it,' he said to Billy. 'Who would have thought that this messy town could change so much? It's a miracle, Billy, that's what it is. You've worked a miracle!'

5. The Great Recycled Cycle Race

Everybody was astonished at how neat the town was looking. And it did seem as if people had changed. They all saved their tins now and Freddy had promised to come back every two weeks to collect them. They were still saving their newspapers, too, which were regularly picked up by Mr Button. The mayor was very pleased by all this and had tried to take most of the credit for it himself. He even asked Ted whether he would like his job back.

'Thank you very much, but no,' said Ted politely. 'I'm happy with my pigs. And anyway, there's hardly any rubbish to sweep up any more now that people are using the rubbish bins.'

Although everybody else seemed to be happy, Billy was not at all satisfied. Although he knew that the town had changed, and was no longer wasteful, he was still ashamed that the outside world thought the town was the dirtiest place in the country.

'We need something to show them that it's all different,' he said to Nicola. As he spoke, the idea came to him. It was a simple idea, but a wonderful one. It would be sure to make the front page of every newspaper in the country, and it would save the town's name. It was a brilliant idea!

Billy had thought of a race. People were always interested in races, and the newspapers certainly liked to report them. This race, though, would be different. It would be a recycling race – a recycled cycle race, to be exact!

Billy explained his idea to Nicola, who thought it was just what was needed.

'This is a race for home-made

bicycles,' he said. 'And every bit of them – every single bit – must be recycled!'

Nicola laughed. 'So if I get hold of some pram wheels and other bits and pieces I could make my own cycle and enter?' she asked.

'Of course,' said Billy. 'You could also use an old wheelbarrow, or an old supermarket trolley, or something like that. The only rule will be that the bike has to be made out of something that somebody else has thrown away.'

This time Billy and Nicola sent a letter to the editor of the local newspaper, who published it on the front page. Everybody who read about it

– or just about everybody – wanted to enter the race.

Over the next few days, any old wheels that were lying about in the town were snapped up. One boy who had failed to find wheels lying about in back lanes had the idea of going fishing. But instead of fish, he caught just what he wanted – a complete set of pram wheels which some lazy – and messy – person had thrown into the town lake. That brought lots of people out with their fishing rods, and soon people had fished up all sorts of interesting things. As well as several old bicycle wheels, people dredged up bits of wire and springs and chains, all of which were to come in handy when it came to building the recycled cycles.

People were very careful to keep their inventions to themselves, and most of the entries were built secretly in garden sheds or garages.

'Have you heard what so-and-so is building?' went the whisper. 'I hear that

it's got five, yes five! wheels and is made entirely out of old pressure cooker lids!'

When at last the day came for the race, the whole town was so excited that everybody was up at six o'clock in the morning, four hours before the great race was due to begin.

As the organisers of the race, Billy and Nicola had a table near the start line. There they issued competitors with their numbers and checked each extraordinary cycle to see that it was made entirely of recycled parts. They had to disqualify some of the entrants, who had bought pieces from shops. But these people were given the chance to act as race officials, so they did not feel too left out.

At last the contestants were lined up at the start line, all fifty of them. And what a peculiar sight it was! There was a cycle made entirely out of bits of wood and scraps of old carpet. There was a cycle made from a gate, with the metal twisted this way and that to get the right shape. A farmer had made his cycle out of old ploughs, and a doctor had blown up the tubes of stethoscopes to make the tyres for his machine! And there was even an old sofa – one of those sofas with little wheels on the legs – which had been turned into a bicycle by a cunning piece of engineering!

Billy gave the mayor a flag to drop when the race began.

'Ladies and gentlemen, er . . . It gives

me great pleasure,' said the mayor. 'Indeed, it gives me very great pleasure to . . . er start . . . er, I mean to begin, or commence this extraordinary race. May I er . . . say that I er . . . feel that this race should do a great deal to . . . er . . .'

'Ready, steady, go!' shouted somebody, who was fed up with waiting for the mayor to get round to starting the race.

Taken by surprise, the mayor dropped the flag and the race began. Off they set, with a great squeaking and creaking, puffing and blowing, and, of course, a great cheering from the crowd.

The race was a long one, and at first the leader was a boy who had built his bicycle out of the wheels of a pram. His machine was light, and it did not take much effort to pedal, but he soon used up all his energy and was overtaken by a girl on a unicycle. It was a most unusual unicycle, though; its single wheel was the wheel of an old sewing machine, and instead of being driven by a chain it was driven by plaited-together rubber bands! But soon she came to a hill and the unicycle went wrong. The rubber bands had somehow got wound up the wrong way and they suddenly whirred off, carrying the girl and her unicycle backwards down the hill and into a pond. Fortunately she was not hurt and was able to laugh at the accident, while she fished the remaining bits of her invention out of the water.

The leader now was a man who had made a tricycle out of a wheelbarrow. He was pedalling away furiously when, suddenly, the bottom fell out of the wheelbarrow and he found himself sitting on the ground, still pedalling, but going nowhere.

There were several other disasters, but luckily nobody was hurt. Then, almost an hour after the race had started, the crowd saw the leaders

racing down the hill towards the finishing line. Everybody shouted lustily, jumping up and down to get a better view of the winner.

It was the sofa! To everybody's surprise, the recycled sofa-cycle had picked up speed, and when it came to the final hill it was positively shooting along.

'It's the sofa-cycle!' people shouted. 'Well done!'

The mayor waved his flag again and people flocked up to the exhausted rider to congratulate him. It had been a great effort, as a sofa is a fairly large thing to ride, and he was very tired. But a few glasses of delicious ice-cold orange juice soon had him feeling much better and ready to receive his prize. Billy was very proud. He had invited one of the best-known racing cyclists in the country to present the prize, and he had agreed.

The famous cyclist smiled as he presented the winner with his trophy. It was, of course, a recycled trophy. Only

the previous day it had been an old vase which somebody had thrown out. Now, neatly painted with silver paint, it was as good as new.

Photographs were taken, and appeared in all the national newspapers the next day, with full reports of the recycled cycle race and how good everybody had been at recycling. Billy was delighted by the attention the race had attracted, and he was thrilled, two days later, when the news came through that the town had won an award for being the best recycling town in the whole country.

The next time that Mr Button came to collect newspapers, he called at Billy's house to congratulate him.

'You're a bit of a genius at recycling,

Billy,' he said. 'You and your sister have cleaned this town up single-handed!'

'I couldn't have done it without your help,' said Billy modestly.

'That may be,' said Mr Button. 'But that brings me round to what I wanted to say. Mr Brace, my partner, and myself are going into business with our friend Freddy Silver. That'll make us the biggest recycling outfit for miles around. And we wondered . . .' he paused here, watching for Billy's reaction. 'We wondered if you and your sister would like to come in on the business with us. Just on Saturdays, of course, since you're still at school. But we're prepared to make you a full member of the business if you wish. You'll come up with the ideas, and we'll carry them out.'

Billy was thrilled.

'Of course I would,' he said. 'That's very kind of you.'

And so they signed an agreement – on recycled paper – and Mr Button tucked it into the pocket of his recycled shirt.

'We've given you a nickname,' he said to Billy. 'I hope you don't mind it. We've been calling you Billy Rubbish.'

Billy laughed. 'That's a good name,' he said, adding: 'I'm sure I'll become rather proud of it!'

And he did.